THE STORY OF DOCTOR DOLITTLE

by HUGH LOFTING

#4 Doctor Dolittle's Magical Cure

Adapted by Diane Namm

Illustrated by John Kanzler

Sterling Publishing Co., Inc.
New York

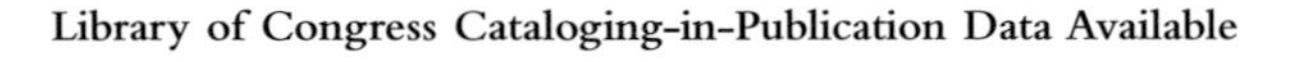

Library of Congress Cataloging-in-Publication Data Available

10 9 8 7 6 5 4 3 2 1

Published by Sterling Publishing Co., Inc.
387 Park Avenue South, New York, NY 10016

Distributed in Canada by Sterling Publishing
c/o Canadian Manda Group, 165 Dufferin Street
Toronto, Ontario, Canada M6K 3H6
Distributed in the United Kingdom by GMC Distribution Services
Castle Place, 166 High Street, Lewes, East Sussex, England BN7 1XU
Distributed in Australia by Capricorn Link (Australia) Pty. Ltd.
P.O. Box 704, Windsor, NSW 2756, Australia

Printed in China

Sterling ISBN-13: 978-1-4027-4123-4
ISBN-10: 1-4027-4123-5

For information about custom editions, special sales, premium and corporate purchases, please contact Sterling Special Sales Department at 800-805-5489 or specialsales@sterlingpub.com.

Contents

Good to Be Home

Circus Crocodile's mother
was happy to have him home.
He had been gone a long time.
"Tell me everything," she said.
"I missed you, Mama, when I
was in Puddleby," he said.
"So we set sail for Africa,"
Doctor Dolittle added.

"There was a terrible storm,"
said Polynesia the parrot.
"We lost our ship and got locked
up," said Chee-Chee the monkey.

"Oh, my," said Mother Crocodile.

"How did you ever find me?"

"A map, of course, and a bit

of luck," Doctor Dolittle said.

Mother Crocodile kissed him
on the nose and said, "Thank you
for bringing my son home."
The doctor turned bright red!

Just then a messenger
arrived from the great lion,
the island's animal king.
"Help!" the message said.

Doctor Dolittle to the Rescue

"The prince cub is very sick," the messenger explained. "The great king lion doesn't know what to do. He has tried everything, but nothing works. The Monkey Council said Doctor Dolittle would have the cure."

"My cures were all lost with our ship," the doctor said. "But we will go at once and see what we can do."

"You'll be right as rain in
no time," the doctor said.
"Stick out your tongue, please."
He took out his viewing glass.
"Aha," said Doctor Dolittle,
"Just as I suspected!"
"Can you cure him?" asked the king.
"Absolutely!" the doctor said.

Doctor Dolittle and the animals looked high and low. "We must find the right plant to make a special brew," he said.

"Will these work?" the animals asked.

The doctor inspected the plants.

"Too leafy. Too brown. Too big.

Too small," he said with a frown.

"Look at that!" the doctor said.

"What?" the animals asked.

They saw no plants at all.

"It's our ship!" the doctor called out.
The animals dragged the ship
to the shore. Doctor Dolittle
found his bag of cures.
"Now we can help!" he said.

Doctor Dolittle gave the
prince cub a spoonful of
this and a spoonful of that.
King Lion waited and watched.

A Pushmi-Pullyu Thank You!

The little prince cub sat up.
He stretched his arms wide.
Then he jumped out of bed.
"I'm all better!" he said.
"Doctor," said the king,
"you're a genius!
How can I repay you?"
"A simple thank you will do,"
Doctor Dolittle told him.

“A royal cure deserves a
royal thank you!” said the king.
“We want you to have our most
favorite thing,” said the prince cub.

“Our pushmi-pullyu!”
said the king lion.
“It never knows if it’s
coming or going!” he said.

"Remarkable!" the doctor said.
"What does a pushmi-pullyu do?"
"I'll show you!" the prince cub said.

“Does it always run in place?”
Doctor Dolittle asked.
“Always!” said the prince cub.
“Amazing!” the doctor said.

"Its wool is magic. It grows all year. It will keep you warm when it's cold, cool when it's hot, and dry when it rains," said the king.

A Sad Good-bye

"It often rains in Puddleby,"
Dab-Dab remembered fondly.
"I miss Puddleby," barked Jip.
"Me, too!" oinked Gub-Gub.
"Well, our work here is done,"
Doctor Dolittle said.
"And our ship is ready,"
the animals reminded him.

"Is there nothing I can say
to keep you here?" asked the king.
"I have patients that need me
in Puddleby," the doctor said.

"Then you must go," the prince said.
"I will send a royal parade
to go with you," said the king.
"You and the animals will
be sent off in style!"

"We have one more thing to do," said the doctor, "We must tell Circus Crocodile good-bye."

"I don't want you to go,"
said Circus Crocodile.
"I like it here," Chee-Chee said.
"Me, too," said Polynesia.

"We don't want to leave," they said.

"Really?" Circus Crocodile asked.

"May we stay?" they asked the doctor.

"Of course," the doctor replied.

"There is just one problem,"
the good doctor said.
"How will we ever get
the pushmi-pullyu aboard?"

The monkeys knew
exactly what to do!
They got the pushmi-pullyu
on the ship in no time at all.

"Good-bye," Doctor Dolittle said,
"Remember to write!"
"Watch out for pirates!" called
the animals from the shore.
"Pirates?" the pushmi-pullyu said.
"Don't worry," said the doctor
as the ship sailed out to sea.
"There are no pirates in Puddleby."